COLORADO SUMMER

COLORADO SUMMER

The story of a Paint named Georgia and the city girl
who strives to make champions of them both

Written by **Larry Bograd & Coleen Hubbard**
Illustrated by **Sandy Rabinowitz**
Cover Illustration by **Christa Keiffer**
Developed by Nancy Hall, Inc.

Gareth Stevens Publishing
MILWAUKEE

For a free color catalog describing Gareth Stevens' list of high-quality books and multimedia programs, call 1-800-542-2595 (USA) or 1-800-461-9120 (Canada). Gareth Stevens Publishing's Fax: (414) 225-0377.

Library of Congress Cataloging-in-Publication Data

Bograd, Larry.
Colorado summer / written by Larry Bograd & Coleen Hubbard;
illustrated by Sandy Rabinowitz; cover illustration by Christa Keiffer.
p. cm.
Originally published: Dyersville, Iowa: Ertl Co., 1997.
(Treasured horses collection)
Summary: Born and bred in New York City, eleven-year-old
Carrie is not looking forward to spending the summer on
her aunt's Colorado ranch until she is introduced to
Georgia, a Paint horse that is as swift as the wind.
ISBN 0-8368-2277-3 (lib. bdg.)
[1. Ranch life—Colorado—Fiction.   2. American paint horse—
Fiction.   3. Horses—Fiction.   4. Colorado—Fiction.]
I. Hubbard, Coleen.   II. Rabinowitz, Sandy, ill.   III. Title.
IV. Series: Treasured horses collection.
PZ7.B635797Co   1999
[Fic]—dc21   98-46294

This edition first published in 1999 by
Gareth Stevens Publishing
1555 North RiverCenter Drive, Suite 201
Milwaukee, Wisconsin 53212 USA

© 1997 by Nancy Hall, Inc.
First published by The ERTL Company, Inc., Dyersville, Iowa.

Treasured Horses Collection is a registered trademark of The ERTL Company, Inc.

Printed in the United States of America

1 2 3 4 5 6 7 8 9 03 02 01 00 99

CONTENTS

Landing in Colorado

"Ladies and gentlemen, we're about to begin our approach to Denver International Airport. Please put your seat in its fully upright position, and be sure that your seat belt is securely fastened."

The voice of the flight attendant startled eleven-year-old Carrie Gordon. She put away the book she was reading and looked out the window. Below her was a wide, dry expanse of land. No wonder they call it the Great Plains, she thought. It's so plain! Nevertheless, Carrie, who had been born and raised in New York City, couldn't take her eyes from the view below. This was her first trip west, and though she'd checked out some books on Colorado from the New York Public Library, she was still surprised at how barren and flat the land looked.

"Be careful," her father had joked, as she boarded the plane. "You might go crazy from too much open space! No tall buildings or crowded streets and subways. No tiny elevators!"

Remembering her father's words made Carrie suddenly homesick. Her stomach clutched and she turned from the window. Not only was she visiting Colorado for the first time, but she was also spending her first summer away from her mom and dad.

Her parents were celebrating their fifteenth wedding anniversary in Europe and were sending Carrie to stay with her great-aunt Mildred. Mildred owned the Western M Ranch that was located on high, arid plains about 100 miles northeast of Denver.

"I'm being banished," Carrie mumbled. She imagined her parents touring London and Paris, seeing great museums, going to the theater, and eating in elegant restaurants. She wanted them to have a great time, but she felt anxious and uncertain about her own summer plans.

The exciting part of the summer, Carrie knew, would be the chance to be around horses and to ride every day. She loved horses and did everything a city girl could do to have them in her life. She went riding in Central Park on weekends and went to a week-long riding camp each summer in upstate New York. She read about horses constantly and had seen every great movie that featured her favorite animal.

But still . . . how would a girl from the big city survive a summer on a remote ranch, where the nearest town had only a few thousand people? And what about Aunt Mildred? Would they get along? Would they find things to talk about? What would it be like to spend so much time with a woman who was seventy years old and had never had children?

Carrie *liked* her great-aunt well enough. At least what she knew of her. Mildred visited the Gordons every other fall in New York to "get a gallon of culture." For a week she would see the latest Broadway shows, spend hours at the art museums and galleries, and take in an opera or symphony. But by the end of the week, she would be tired of the noise and crowds and would tell Carrie that she was ready to head back to her "quiet life under the big sky."

During Mildred's visits, Carrie typically was in school all day. Mostly Mildred went places with Carrie's mom, who was Mildred's niece. But in the evening everyone would have dinner together, and Mildred would tell wonderful stories about her horses.

Mildred was full of energy and humor, especially

when she talked about her horses and the ranch. But to Carrie, the Western M sounded like something out of an old cowboy movie, almost as foreign as living in another country. Still, she would listen eagerly to her aunt's stories and picture herself riding bareback across a windswept prairie—just like in the movies.

Mildred would end each of her trips to the Big Apple with an invitation for Carrie to come west for a visit some day.

Now that day had arrived. Carrie couldn't quite believe it. To make it seem more real, she reached into her purple backpack and pulled out a handful of photos that Mildred had sent to her. Each of the pictures featured one of the horses Mildred kept on the ranch. On the back of each was a name and a description of the animal, scrawled in blue ink by her aunt.

The first horse was Mildred's old companion, a Palomino named Casey. Then came Buckeroo Bob, an Appaloosa who belonged to Mildred's late husband, Donald. Carrie had never met Uncle Donald because he had died when she was two. It was strange to think of Aunt Mildred living alone for so many years, with just her horses and a few hired hands for company.

Carrie studied the next snapshot, which showed a pair of draft horses named Fred and Barney. "Their working days are over," said the note on the back. "But they still pull the hay wagon for town parades."

The final photo was Carrie's favorite. She had been staring at it for weeks. She had even taped it to the wall next to her bed. The horse was a beautiful six-year-old Paint named Georgia, after the famous American painter Georgia O'Keeffe.

Georgia's coat was a warm brown with what looked like white paint poured over her back. Her legs were dark with white stockings, and her face had a stripe of white. The contrast between her dark coat and white markings gave her a striking appearance.

Carrie thought she had never seen a finer horse. The mare looked strong and muscular, with a spirited intelligence to her eyes. Carrie couldn't wait to ride her! She turned the photo over to read her aunt's inscription. "Georgia," it said. "A real western horse for my 'eastern' niece. She's as fast as the wind!"

Carrie closed her eyes and imagined herself and Georgia galloping across her aunt's ranch, with miles and miles of open land to explore. She felt the sun on her face, and her hands confidently guiding the reins. For a moment she was lost in her wonderful fantasy and forgot about missing her parents. She even forgot her worries about Aunt Mildred and the long, long summer ahead.

Suddenly the jet banked sharply to the left, and Carrie snapped open her eyes. Right below the tipped wing was the Denver airport, with its white peaked roof designed to look like the snow-capped Rocky Mountains. The Captain announced the final approach, and within minutes the airplane was speeding to a halt on the runway.

Carrie took a deep breath. This is it, she thought. My adventure begins. She took one last look at Georgia and then put the photos away. She found her hairbrush in her backpack and gave her tangled, layered black hair a quick brushing. Then she tucked her white t-shirt into her jeans and retied the laces on her black, high-top sneakers.

I wonder if Mildred will recognize me? Carrie thought, as the airplane taxied to the gate. It had been two years since Mildred had been to New York, and Carrie had grown five inches during that time.

Her mother had assured Carrie that she bore a family resemblance to her great-aunt. "You have the same hazel-colored eyes and high cheekbones," she had told Carrie, "and you're both tall. She'll spot you in a minute."

Carrie hoped so, because the plane had stopped at the gate. All around her passengers groped for their belongings and edged their way into the crowded aisle. Carrie slipped her backpack over one shoulder and reached beneath her seat for two packages. They were gifts for Mildred from her parents: a new biography of Georgia O'Keeffe—the painter—and a dozen egg bagels from New York City, bought fresh that morning.

Carrie walked through the jetway, looking right and left for Mildred. After a few seconds she spotted her, waving enthusiastically from the back of the crowd.

Mildred made her way to Carrie and gave her a hearty hug. "Welcome to Colorado!" she said. "You must have grown five inches!"

"Five inches exactly," Carrie laughed.

"Let me look at you," Mildred said, putting her hands on Carrie's shoulders. "Why, you're the spitting image of your mother at this age," she declared, shaking her head. "Except for that sophisticated city attitude you can't help but have." Mildred laughed a warm, throaty laugh and winked at Carrie.

Carrie was impressed at how well her aunt looked for being seventy and spending almost her entire life as a rancher. Her face was weathered, but she carried herself with regal pride. She's not embarrassed to be tall, Carrie thought. She likes it.

Mildred was dressed in a long, cotton print skirt, a western-style blouse, and cowboy boots with a rounded toe. Her long, gray hair was pulled back with a large, Navajo, turquoise barrette.

"Let's go get your suitcases," Mildred said, steering Carrie down a shiny, unending corridor.

"I only brought one," Carrie said. "I like to travel light."

"Me too," said Mildred. "You're my kind of traveler."

"Mom said you have a washing machine."

"I sure do," Mildred responded. "But the dryer's gone on strike. We'll have to hang everything out on the line in the sun to dry."

Carrie laughed at this idea. She had never in her life hung laundry out to dry. In the basement of the apartment building where her family lived, they fed quarters into a long row of washers and dryers and went up and down in the elevator between loads.

While they waited at the baggage claim for Carrie's suitcase, she remembered the gifts.

"These are from Mom and Dad," Carrie said,

handing over the book. "For taking care of me."

"Nonsense," answered Mildred. "I should be sending *them* a gift for letting me have you this summer. You're a breath of fresh air to a lonesome old lady like me."

Next Carrie gave her the lumpy brown bag of bagels, tied with a red ribbon. Her aunt laughed and held the package up to her nose. "If I know your mother, these are egg bagels from that place on your street corner."

"You got it," Carrie said.

"You can't get bagels in this part of the world, I'm warning you right now."

"I'll try to survive," Carrie said. She was already feeling comfortable with her aunt. Mildred had an easy way about her, and a nice sense of humor. Carrie was dying to ask her about Georgia and the other horses, but she decided to wait until they began the long drive to the ranch.

While they waited, Mildred paged through the art book and sighed in appreciation. "I do love Georgia O'Keeffe. What a wonderful painter."

Carrie couldn't resist. "Speaking of Georgia . . ." she began, clearing her throat.

"I was wondering when you were going to ask," laughed Mildred. "I thought maybe you weren't interested in horses anymore."

"Oh, no!" Carrie exclaimed. "I love horses. I was trying to be polite."

"Well, do me a favor, Carrie," Mildred said.

"What?" asked Carrie.

"Try not to be too polite this summer, okay? I get nervous when folks are too polite."

"It's a deal," said Carrie. "So tell me all about Georgia."

"Georgia is doing just fine," said Mildred. "Except for one big problem."

Carrie's heart pounded. "What?" she asked, fearing something terrible.

"She's suffering from a lack of attention. With just me and two hired hands to care for the ranch and the animals, she just doesn't get enough love."

Carrie breathed a sigh of relief. Georgia was fine. And Georgia needed her.

"I can help with that," Carrie said. "I can give her all the attention she needs." At that moment, Carrie spotted her black canvas suitcase and grabbed it from the carousel.

"Well then," said Mildred, pointing toward an exit door, "let's get going. Let's get the two of you properly introduced!"

Dressing Like a Local

"**H**ave you been riding much, Carrie?" Mildred asked.

Carrie turned to her aunt, who was steering her old red pickup truck out of the city limits of Denver. They were headed north and east across the Great Plains.

"Every chance I get," Carrie replied. "Mostly weekends in Central Park. Mom and I rent horses or take a lesson."

"Have you run over any joggers yet?" Mildred joked.

"Not yet," said Carrie. "But you do have to be careful to avoid all the people and strollers and bicycles. And then there are the skaters!"

"Well, you won't have that trouble on the ranch. You can ride all day and not see another soul."

"I can't wait!" Carrie thought again about riding Georgia fast and hard across the prairie. It made her skin tingle with anticipation.

"Of course, you might run into my hired hands. Warren O'Connell and his son, Daniel."

Carrie paused for a moment, then asked her aunt what she hoped wasn't too silly a question. "Aunt Mildred, exactly what does a hired hand do? They always have them in western movies."

Mildred smiled at Carrie. "I like people who ask a question when they don't know something. That's a good trait to have."

"I'm glad you think so," Carrie said. "Because there's so much I don't know about ranches and horses and all of this."

Carrie gestured out the window at the flat, open land broken only by the two-lane highway they were driving.

"You'll be an expert come August, I promise," Mildred said. "You have this land in your blood. You just don't know it yet. Your people come from here. In fact, your mother was one of the few who ever escaped!"

Carrie wondered if that were true. Could someone be related to a place the way they were related to a person? Could a girl be from New York and still feel a pull toward Colorado, a place she'd never even visited?

Mildred interrupted Carrie's thoughts. "Now there I go, forgetting to answer your question about hired hands. Warren O'Connell has a chicken farm not far from the ranch, and Daniel is his grown son. They help me with the horses, and mend fences, and whatever else needs to be done. You'll soon see that the Western M needs a lot of help."

"What do you mean?" asked Carrie.

"Well, I'm not getting any younger. Some days I wake up and think of selling the place. You see, a ranch is like a living thing. It needs constant tending. The land, the animals, the buildings—all of it."

Thinking about the ranch being sold made Carrie feel sad—though she wasn't exactly sure why. She hadn't even seen it, yet. The two of them sat in silence for a few minutes. Carrie was beginning to feel hungry and tired, and she was anxious to get to the ranch.

"Now, if my memory serves," said Mildred, breaking the silence, "you ride English style, don't you?"

"That's all I know," Carrie replied.

"So you probably only have English riding boots."

"Yes, but I didn't bring them. I didn't think they'd be the right kind for the west. Mom and Dad gave me money to buy boots and whatever else you think I need."

"Well, then, I think we should plan on stopping in Yuma."

"Where's Yuma?" asked Carrie.

"Up the road. Our version of a big city. We can have a late lunch there and pick up what we need."

A half hour later they passed a sign that read, "Welcome to Yuma, Colorado. Yu-ma have the time of your life!"

Carrie couldn't believe how tiny the town was. It looked like a movie set, with its one main street running parallel to some railroad tracks, and hardly a tree in sight.

"Different from home, huh?" Mildred asked as she watched Carrie gape at the small, dusty town.

"You can say that again!" exclaimed Carrie. "No taxi cabs, no traffic jams, no hoards of people . . ."

"No tall buildings," added Mildred. "Unless you count the grain elevator, which is about four stories high."

"That's five stories *shorter* than our apartment

building. Can I take a picture, Aunt Mildred?"

Mildred slowed the truck to a stop while Carrie dug in her backpack for her small, automatic camera. She leaned out the window and focused on the white tower of the grain elevator. Then she snapped a picture of Main Street.

"I promised Mom and Dad I'd take a picture of everything."

"You're off to a good start," said Mildred. "Let's go get some lunch. I'm starving."

"Me too," Carrie said, clutching her stomach. "I didn't eat on the plane. I was too nervous."

"The Broken Wheel Cafe is right across the road. They make a mean grilled-cheese-and-tomato sandwich and the best milk shakes in the county."

"Do they make onion rings?" asked Carrie, hopefully. Onion rings were one of her favorite things to eat.

"Absolutely! And you can meet my old friend, Frankie, who owns the place. She's the best cook in the county."

Mildred was right, Carrie thought, as she gobbled her sandwich, shake, and crispy onion rings. Frankie was a terrific cook. And she was nice, too. Short and plump with a long white ponytail, she teased Carrie about being from New York.

22

"But at least you appreciate good food," Frankie said with a laugh. "And you have a healthy appetite, just like your aunt!"

After lunch, Mildred and Carrie walked down the sidewalk to Norman's, which sold boots, saddles, and western attire. Mildred explained that Carrie would need roper boots, like the ones she was wearing.

"The toe is rounded for comfort, and the heel is lower than your usual cowboy boot. You're on your feet a lot on a ranch."

Carrie thought they looked a little funny. Once she tried on a pair, though, she had to admit they were comfortable. She walked around the store, touching the western-style saddles and the assortment of bridles.

"You'll need a hat, too. Straw with a full brim for summer," said Mildred. "Keeps the sun off your face but lets some air through."

By the time they were finished shopping, Carrie hardly recognized herself. When she looked in the store mirror, the only familiar thing was her old pair of blue jeans. Besides the boots and hat, she was now wearing a blue denim western shirt, a red bandanna, and a pair of sturdy work gloves made of leather.

"I look like I'm in a movie," Carrie marveled. "No one at home would recognize me now." She thought briefly about her friends at home, who were probably wearing short summer skirts and fashionable sandals with straps and buckles.

"You look like a girl who is ready to work hard and ride hard," said Mildred. "If you walked down Main Street right now, folks would think you were a local."

"Can we go to the ranch now?" Carrie asked. The shopping was fun, but she was afraid if they didn't hurry the whole day would be gone before she had a chance to finally meet her Paint.

"Soon as I pay up," said Mildred. Mildred insisted on paying for the purchases, even though Carrie had brought more than enough money to cover the cost. She pushed aside Carrie's wallet with stubborn pride. "This is my treat, and I won't hear another word about it."

Carrie laughed and Mildred gave her a wondering look. "What's so funny?" she asked.

"Mom warned me," Carrie answered, "that you could be pretty stubborn."

"Really?" said Mildred, as she gave the cashier a check. "Your mother told me the same thing about you. She said when you get a thought in your head, there isn't anything in the world that can distract you from it."

"I guess she's right," Carrie admitted. "Right now all I can think about is—"

"Let me see," Mildred interrupted. "Georgia?"

"You guessed it. Will I meet her before dark?"

"Absolutely," said Mildred. "Not much traffic from here to the Western M. Just an old dirt road."

Carrie and Mildred left Norman's and headed for the red pickup. Carrie was thinking how strange it was to be in a town with no video store, no compact disc store, no Chinese nor Indian restaurants, no art galleries nor coffee bars. I don't fit in here, Carrie thought, looking down at her new boots.

But anyone passing the two of them on the main street of Yuma would merely notice an older woman and a young girl, both tall, both wearing similar boots and hats, both walking with quick purpose and heads held high.

Georgia on My Mind

66There it is," Mildred said to Carrie as they turned off the dirt road and onto a long, straight driveway. "There's the Western M Ranch."

Carrie sat forward with excitement. "Finally!" she said. Finally she would meet Georgia and begin her summer adventure in Colorado.

Inside the barbed wire fence, Carrie could see the modest ranch house and several old buildings. The house itself was built in 1907, with a peaked roof and white pillars across the front. Carrie noticed that it needed a fresh coat of paint, but thought it had an old-fashioned charm. She liked the black shutters and the red front door.

Beyond the house was an old chicken coop, the barn, and a storage shed, all painted a fading red. Carrie realized that the buildings did need fixing up.

"Over there," said Mildred, pointing to a group of buildings made of rough logs, "is the bunk house, the tack house, and the corral. Of course the bunk house is empty now, but . . ."

Carrie had stopped listening the minute she spotted the corral. It was empty at the moment, but just being near it made her happy. Georgia must be in the barn, she decided. Carrie wondered if she could go see the horses first thing.

Mildred must have read her mind, for when she stopped the truck she said, "Why don't you hop out and head over to the barn. I'll meet you in a bit. I need to freshen up after that dusty drive."

Carrie slammed the door of the truck and practically ran to the barn. She found Georgia immediately. The horse was leaning her muscular neck over the stall door. Even though Carrie longed to run up and throw her arms around the horse's neck, she controlled herself. She didn't want to startle Georgia on their first meeting. So she stood against the barn door and watched Georgia for a moment.

"You're prettier than your picture," Carrie called out softly. Georgia arched her neck and pricked her ears forward. Her face and eyes looked friendly, so Carrie figured it was fine to move closer. She held out her hand, palm up, and Georgia sniffed it and nickered. Carrie was delighted by the greeting and stroked the horse's beautiful brown and white coat.

"Nice to finally meet you," Carrie said. "I've been waiting for weeks."

Then Carrie heard someone come into the barn. She turned around and saw Mildred. "It looks as though she likes you."

"Do you think so?" Carrie asked.

"She doesn't come up to just anyone. She likes to be moving—and moving fast!

"Who usually rides her?" asked Carrie. "Do you?"

"Sometimes," Mildred answered. "But most days my arthritis keeps me away. My hired hand—Warren—has a daughter in college. She used to come over and work the barrels with Georgia, but she's working at a dude ranch this summer. Mostly, Warren or Daniel give her some exercise."

"What do you mean, work the barrels?" Carrie asked.

"Oh, my heavens, I guess I forgot to tell you that this horse was born and bred to be a barrel racer."

"You mean for rodeos?" Carrie asked.

"Yes, ma'am. Her great-great grandma was a

champion. Lucinda was her name. Took first place four years in a row, way back before you were born."

"Who rode Lucinda?" Carrie asked, becoming more curious by the minute.

"Why, I did," Mildred said, grinning at Carrie and moving forward to pat Georgia.

"You were a barrel racer? How come you never talked about that?"

"Oh, I guess I don't much like to talk about myself," said Mildred. "I'd rather hear about other folks. Besides, that's in the past, when I was young. I'm an old lady now."

Carrie shook her head in wonder. She tried to picture her great-aunt speeding around barrels at a rodeo and winning first prize. She realized there was much more to Mildred than she knew.

"You want to ride her?" Mildred asked, nodding toward Georgia.

"Can I?"

"Let's get her tacked up and give it a try."

In the tack room, Mildred chose a bridle and saddle for Carrie to use. The equipment looked different from the kind Carrie used to ride English style.

"The western saddle," Mildred explained, "was developed to handle all the kinds of work cowboys

and cowgirls do on a ranch—riding, roping, cutting.
See the horn, the handle there at the front? That's
where you would tie your lasso."

Carrie laughed at this. "I guess I probably won't
be learning to use a lasso quite yet."

Mildred helped Carrie adjust the bit and showed
her how to put the saddle on Georgia. "In English
riding you use a girth to hold the saddle in place," she
told Carrie. "We western riders call it a cinch."

Then Carrie led her horse out to the corral. She
talked gently to Georgia, but mostly to calm her own
racing heart.

Inside the corral were three steel barrels set in a
triangle formation. The instant Georgia saw them, she
shook her mane and stamped at the ground.

"She's ready to go," Mildred said. "She loves the
barrels. And she has the heart for competition. But for
now, Georgia, why don't you be a proper host and
give our guest a spin around the ring?"

Carrie mounted Georgia and shifted her weight in
the saddle, which felt strange at first. She tried not to
let the horse or Mildred know that she was nervous.
Relax and be in control, she told herself. Soon they
were jogging at a steady pace. Carrie knew that
western riders don't post the way she was used to
doing in Central Park. At first she was afraid she

would bounce, but Georgia's jog was so smooth, she had no trouble sitting to it.

"What a wonderful horse!" Carrie shouted. Georgia was, indeed, quick and responsive, and Carrie felt as though she'd been riding her for years instead of minutes.

"You look good," Mildred called back. "Those New York horse folks have taught you well."

As Carrie continued to ride, she felt happier than she had in a long time. The sun was just beginning to set in the west, and a slight breeze ruffled her hair. The smell of cut hay and prairie sage filled the air. The only sounds came from some far off crickets and Georgia's hooves as they hit the dirt.

Carrie took a deep breath and smiled. For the first time, she noticed that the land was actually pretty, and not just flat and brown. The ache in her heart for her parents and home seemed to fade a tiny bit.

"You should cool her down," Mildred suggested. "We need to think about eating dinner and getting you settled."

Carrie didn't want to stop, but she obeyed her aunt. She slowed Georgia to a walk, talking to her softly. "Good girl, Georgia. Thanks for the ride."

Carrie dismounted and began to lead Georgia out of the corral, when she suddenly turned back and looked at her aunt. An unexpected desire rose up in her. "Could I try the barrels?" she asked. "Just once?"

"The barrels? Aren't you getting hungry?"

"Please?" Carrie asked. "Just for a minute?"

"There's that stubborn streak," Mildred said, winking. "Barrel racing takes a long time to learn. There are a lot of steps involved."

"Just show me the first one, then," said Carrie.

Mildred looked steadily at Carrie, as if she were trying to make up her mind.

"It's been a long time since I taught anyone," she said finally.

"But it's in your blood," Carrie insisted. "Just like you told me this land is in *my* blood."

"Okay. One lesson before supper. Here, let me show you."

Mildred mounted Georgia and walked the cloverleaf pattern around the three barrels, explaining as she went along.

"First of all," Mildred said, "you have to learn how to use the reins western style. Hold them in your left hand, and steer Georgia by touching her neck with the rein so that she turns away from it."

"That looks hard," Carrie said. "I'm used to English style where you use both hands."

Mildred continued her lesson. "Basically, barrel

racing is a test of speed and agility. Good horses travel at twenty to thirty miles an hour and a good run is about fourteen to eighteen seconds for a professional rider."

"Wow!" said Carrie, imagining she and Georgia spinning around the barrels.

"You can start with the right barrel or the left

barrel," Mildred continued. "You have 60 feet between the timer line and the first barrel, 90 feet between the first and second barrel, and 105 feet between the second and third barrel."

"What if the horse touches a barrel?" Carrie asked.

"You aren't penalized," Mildred explained, "but if you knock one over it costs you five seconds."

"What makes Georgia a good horse for barrel racing?" Carrie asked.

"Well, Georgia is well trained. She's tight around the turns, and she can really go fast for the finish."

"Can I try?" Carrie asked.

"Your turn," Mildred answered, dismounting Georgia.

Carrie mounted and practiced holding the reins in her left hand. She walked Georgia around the barrels, trying to guide her by neck reining. It felt strange, as though she had less control of her horse than when she rode English.

"This feels weird," Carrie said. She wanted Georgia to turn left around the barrel, but she got mixed up and had her turning away and to the right of the barrel.

"You'll get used to it," Mildred said, encouragingly.

After they went several times around the barrels at a walk, Carrie relaxed. The reining began to feel more natural. "This is fun!" she called, slowing Georgia to a stop.

Just then Georgia twisted her head around and tried to bite at the reins.

"What was that about?" Carrie cried out.

Mildred laughed. "She's bored, I think. She could walk these barrels in her sleep. And you can't have that much slack in the reins, honey."

Carrie laughed, too, but she felt a bit embarrassed. There was so much she didn't know.

"That's enough of a lesson for one day," Mildred said. "Next time be sure to show Georgia you're the one in control."

As they headed back to the barn, Carrie asked, "How did barrel racing become a rodeo event, Aunt Mildred?"

"That's a good story," Mildred chuckled. "And a long one. I'll tell you after dinner."

CHAPTER FOUR

Under the Stars

"I'll do the dishes," Carrie told Mildred. They had just finished their dinner of cold chicken, corn on the cob, and fresh, sliced tomatoes. A peach cobbler was cooling on the kitchen counter.

"We'll take turns during your stay," Mildred said. "I have a few calls to make in my study, so we'll have dessert in half an hour."

Alone in the kitchen, Carrie's thoughts returned to Georgia and her first lesson in barrel racing. What a day it had been! It was hard to believe that she had been in Colorado only since the morning.

After the dishes were dried and put away, Carrie

wandered around the house. She loved the living room with its high ceiling and stone fireplace. In one corner was an ancient, black-and-white television. But there was no computer nor VCR, no CD player, and certainly no cable channels on the television.

Carrie felt cut off from the rest of the world. Restless, she wandered to the back bedroom, which would be hers for the summer. It had old bunk beds with red-and-yellow plaid blankets, a desk with a lamp, a straight-backed rocking chair, and several paintings of western landscapes on the walls.

Carrie studied one of the paintings closely. It looked very much like the view Carrie had seen while riding Georgia in the corral. It showed a prairie sunset with pink and yellow clouds. In the bottom corner was the artist's signature. Carrie could barely read it, but after a few seconds she realized it said Mildred Wilson. Her aunt seemed to have quite a few hidden talents.

Carrie returned to the living room and found her aunt making a fire in the stone fireplace.

"A fire, how nice!" said Carrie. She sat down on a soft, brown leather sofa.

"The wonderful thing about this part of the country," said Mildred, "is that no matter how hot it gets in the daytime, the air gets downright chilly at night."

"In New York in the summer," said Carrie, "I think it actually gets hotter at night, and the air can be so sticky. I won't miss *that*."

"If you get cold tonight, there are extra blankets in your closet," said Mildred. The fire was burning nicely, so she joined Carrie on the sofa. "Is your room all right for you? Do you have everything you need?"

"I'm fine," Carrie said, "but I think I might be too excited to sleep tonight."

"You can always go out and look at the stars," said Mildred. "I do that sometimes when I can't sleep."

Carrie was eager to change the subject. She didn't want to think about sleep, yet. "You promised you'd tell me all about barrel racing," she said. "Do you have any pictures of you as a competitor?"

"I have some old scrapbooks, but are you sure you want to spend your evening looking through those musty old things?"

"More than anything!" Carrie said.

Mildred went over to a battered wooden trunk in the corner of the room and lifted the heavy lid. After digging around for a few minutes, she pulled out a stack of cloth covered scrapbooks. She brought them over and put them on the coffee table in front of Carrie.

"Sure you don't want some of that peach cobbler first?"

39

"No," said Carrie. "Remember how stubborn I can be?"

"I remember," Mildred laughed. She opened the first scrapbook and blew some dust from the pages. "There I am," she said, pointing to a photograph.

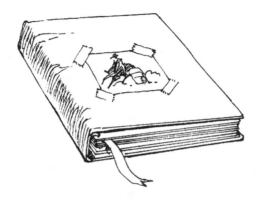

Carrie caught her breath. It was so amazing to see her aunt as a young woman, sitting proudly on a horse. "You look beautiful!" she said.

"Me or the horse?" asked Mildred with a big grin.

"Both of you, actually. Is that Georgia's ancestor?"

"No, honey. That was a horse named Flame. See the white marking on his face? Looks like a flame."

"When was this taken?" Carrie asked.

"That was the late 1940s. I lived in Texas then. There was a group of Texas ranch women who wanted a rodeo event all their own. So we began the sport of barrel racing."

"Do men ever compete?" asked Carrie, still studying the picture.

"Not on the professional level. It's one of the few sports reserved for women."

"That's so neat!" exclaimed Carrie. "That makes me like it even more. At school I play on a girl's soccer team, and we have a great time together."

"I made some wonderful friends through the sport," said Mildred. "There were some terrific women involved back then, just as there are some terrific ones now."

"Do you keep in touch with any of them?"

"Well," said Mildred, shaking her head, "it's been almost ten years since I've seen my rodeo friends. Lots of them came to your Uncle Donald's funeral, but time passes and folks are busy . . . ."

"How did you meet Uncle Donald?" Carrie asked. "Was he involved in the rodeo, too?"

"Oh, yes! He was on the pro circuit when I was. We met in Kansas, right after I won second place at the Wichita State Fair. He came right up to me and asked me to have a root beer with him. It was love at first sight."

"And then you moved here?"

"After we were married, we moved back to Colorado and bought the Western M. I was born near here, and I always wanted to come back."

"Did you keep competing?" Carrie asked. She worried that her endless questions were bothering Mildred, but she wanted to know everything.

"Sure did. For a while. To tell you the truth, though, barrel racing is a sport for young women. Young women with strong bones and a lot of energy."

"Can I ask you one more question?" Carrie asked.

"You can ask me a hundred."

"Did you ever hear of anyone who became a barrel racer who didn't grow up with horses? Or live in the country?"

Mildred looked at Carrie with a steady gaze. "Are you asking me if a girl from the city can learn the sport and excel at it?"

Carrie felt her cheeks flush, but she kept her eyes on her aunt. "That's what I'm asking," she said.

"Well, honey, I think that any girl with courage and endurance and an instinct for horses can certainly learn the sport. But there needs to be an excellent match between the horse and the rider. Both need to want to win."

Carrie was silent. She continued to page through the scrapbook.

"That woman there," said Mildred, pointing to a picture of a woman with long braids, "was my best friend. Delores DeHart. I haven't heard from her in years, but I hear she owns several riding schools around the country. She's done very well."

Carrie was so interested in the photos that she didn't even notice when Mildred got up to dish out peach cobbler. She loved looking at the pictures and the yellowing scraps of newspaper. She especially loved a group photo she found of Mildred and her barrel-racing friends. They were all sitting on a corral fence with their hats in their hands. Their hair blew around their faces and their eyes were shining.

"Let's have our cobbler," Mildred said, sliding next to Carrie with two plates and two forks. "Then I'm going to get my beauty sleep."

"Yum," said Carrie, tasting the sweet, warm peaches. "This is delicious."

"In the morning you can help me muck out the stables," said Mildred. "How's that for an offer?"

"It's a deal," said Carrie. "But you'll have to show me how."

After Mildred said goodnight and went into her bedroom, Carrie finished looking through the scrapbooks. She looked at her watch and realized it was almost ten o'clock. That meant it was almost midnight in New York. And almost breakfast time in Paris, where her parents were.

Though her body was tired, Carrie's mind was still racing. How would she learn barrel racing in one summer? Would she and Georgia be a good match?

Thinking of Georgia made Carrie even more restless. She decided to go out and look at the stars as Mildred had suggested earlier. The back screen door squeaked as she went out. Carrie hoped she wouldn't wake her aunt.

She walked away from the house and headed instinctively toward the barn. Without thinking, she quietly unlatched the barn door and stepped inside. She loved the way the barn smelled—horses, hay, and weathered wood. It was dark, and Carrie realized she didn't know where the light switch was. The moonlight filtering through the boards of the barn provided enough light that she could see the outline of Georgia's head. She didn't want to disturb the animals, so she blew a goodnight kiss in Georgia's direction.

"See you in the morning," she whispered. "Sweet dreams."

Carrie left the barn and headed back to the house. Right before she went inside, she remembered to look up at the stars.

"Oh, my," she breathed, staring at the vivid Milky Way loaded with bright stars. It looked to her as though there were at least a million of them, all twinkling in the black night.

Suddenly, a shooting star shot across the sky. It gave a quick burst of light and faded. Carrie squeezed her eyes shut and made her wish.

"I wish that Georgia and I become a champion barrel-racing team!"

Ranch Life

After Mildred finished her second cup of coffee and Carrie finished her third piece of toast and honey, the two of them went out to the barn. Although the sun had been up for less than an hour, Mildred's hired hands were already at work.

"Warren and Daniel," said Mildred, "I'd like to introduce you to my great-niece, Carrie Gordon. She'll be with me for most of the summer."

Carrie smiled, and they politely tipped their hats to her.

"I think Carrie might make your life a little bit easier, Daniel, because she wants to take over caring for Georgia this summer," said Mildred.

"Once you show me how," Carrie added quickly.

"She's a great horse," said Warren. "My daughter took quite a liking to her."

"Well, why don't you come with me," said Daniel, who had a nice smile and curly dark hair. "I'll show you how to get started."

"Thanks, Daniel," said Mildred. "Warren, shall you and I figure out our hay and feed order?"

Daniel and Carrie went to Georgia's stall. Carrie said good morning to her, and Georgia snorted playfully in return.

"She's trying to be patient," said Daniel, "but she's eager for exercise. She's had her breakfast, so now we need to groom her and clean her stall. I'm going to let her run in the corral while we clean up."

Carrie wanted to go with Georgia, but she knew it was important to learn the chores she would have to perform. Daniel showed her how to muck out the stall and put in clean straw. They also scrubbed out the water bucket and refilled it with fresh water from the pump. Finally, Daniel led Georgia back to her clean stall.

Georgia took a long drink of water and nosed around in the new straw. "She's just arranging her home," Daniel joked. Then he brought out the curry comb and brushes and showed Carrie how to get the dirt out of Georgia's skin and hair. Carrie gave Georgia's white stockings extra attention, so they practically gleamed.

Georgia seemed to like her grooming. She stretched her neck forward in pleasure, wiggling her lips whenever Daniel rubbed an itchy spot.

"You must stay very busy," Carrie said, watching how hard Daniel worked.

"We do," he agreed, "between our chickens and Mildred's horses. Horses are more fun than chickens, though. I love riding them and taking care of them."

"Me too," said Carrie. Georgia's coat now shone, and the contrast between her white and brown areas was even more striking. Her mane and tail felt soft and silky.

"Well, she's all yours," Daniel said. "You know what this horse could really use?" he added. "A long ride outside the corral. Really let her stretch her legs. She's fast, and she needs a fast rider.

Carrie thanked him for his help and went to find her aunt, hoping for a second lesson in barrel racing.

Mildred was finished with her feed order, so she and Carrie agreed to meet in the corral for a short lesson.

"A horse is really only good for about fifteen minutes of concentrated practice on something she already knows," Mildred explained. "So we'll start with short lessons."

Once inside the corral, Georgia immediately began to stamp her right front foot.

"She's excited to start work," Mildred observed.

"So am I," Carrie said.

They began the lesson by having Carrie mount and walk Georgia through the cloverleaf pattern, just like before. This time it was much easier for Carrie to guide Georgia with the reins in one hand.

Then Mildred told her to work up to a jog. This worried Carrie. She didn't want to embarrass herself by knocking over a barrel.

"Don't be afraid," Mildred said, sensing her uneasiness. "When you learn barrel racing, you can be sure you're going to knock over a whole bunch of barrels every day!"

Carrie took a deep breath and took off. She was crazy to have ever thought that barrel racing was simple! But at least she had a great teacher and a smart, fast horse.

Together, Carrie and Georgia repeated the pattern a half dozen times. Sometimes they knocked over one or two barrels. Sometimes, though, they made it around all three.

"Going fast and staying in control is hard!" Carrie

exclaimed, wiping her brow.

"Wait till you learn to drive a car," Mildred joked.

For the final part of the lesson, Mildred had Carrie stop Georgia about ten feet before each of the three barrels.

"What's this for?" Carrie asked.

"You're learning to make a pocket."

"A pocket?" asked Carrie, confused.

"The turning area between the horse and the barrel. Here, let me show you."

Carrie dismounted, trading places with Mildred. She sat on the fence and watched as Mildred took the barrels at an even jog. As she rode, she explained, "You don't have to worry about speed for now. That's for later. Now, I want you to jog up to the first barrel, from the right, and leave lots of pocket, like this. Then head for the second barrel. It should look like I'm going to run into it, but when I get ten feet from it, like this, I shift my weight to the outside stirrup, I apply pressure with my left leg, and Georgia begins to make the pocket."

Mildred made it look so easy. As she rode, years seemed to shed from her body. As Mildred sat high in the saddle, guiding Georgia with ease, Carrie saw a glimmer of the former champion. Her affection for her aunt grew even more in those moments of watching her. Carrie's appreciation for Georgia deepened, too, as she saw the agile, smart horse respond to Mildred.

Mildred slowed Georgia and brought her over to the fence next to Carrie. Carrie reached out to stroke Georgia's neck. She looked proud, with her ears forward and her nostrils flared. Her tail was high, and she flipped her head once in Carrie's direction.

"You're amazing, Aunt Mildred!" Carrie said. "You made it look so easy."

"Thanks, honey," Mildred responded. "I have to admit that your enthusiasm about learning the barrels has rekindled a bit of my old spark."

Warren appeared at the fence and took the reins as Mildred dismounted. "Nice to see you up there riding, Mildred," he said.

"Nothing like a little spur from the younger generation to bring out the best in us old folks, right?" Mildred kidded with Warren.

Back at the house, Mildred asked Carrie if she would like to drive into Yuma with her later in the afternoon. "I need to pick up the feed and some other supplies," she explained. "You might enjoy an ice-cream cone at the Dairy Barn."

"What I would really like," said Carrie, "is to take Georgia out later for a long ride around the ranch. Daniel said she needs to stretch her legs."

"That's true," Mildred agreed. "And I haven't shown you much of the ranch yet. Why don't we both go? I'll pick up the feed and supplies tomorrow."

"Oh, thank you!" cried Carrie.

"First I need to call the weather information line and hear if there are any storms gathering this afternoon."

"Why?" asked Carrie.

"Around here, summer weather can sneak right up on you in the afternoons. You have to be careful. In fact, a twister landed not eight miles from here just last week and caused all sorts of damage."

Mildred made her call and said it was safe for them to ride, but they would have to wait until after lunch. That seemed like forever to Carrie, but it was only two hours.

Carrie managed to pass the time by napping a little and writing quick notes to her parents and her friends at home. She even helped her aunt pull weeds from between the bean plants. They ate their noon meal on a picnic table outside.

And then, finally, it was time to saddle Georgia, and Casey, Mildred's Palomino.

As they prepared to leave, her aunt reminded her to watch the sky for bad weather and to be careful of the barbed wire fences. She also told Carrie not to be

surprised if they saw a rabbit, a prairie dog, or even
an occasional harmless snake.

The two of them set off on their horses, jogging
north of the barn, talking as they went. Mildred
pointed out all kinds of interesting things, like an old
well, a cottonwood tree that had been struck by
lightning, and the remains of an ancient cabin that
had been on the land since before Mildred bought it.

Carrie could hardly believe how huge the ranch
was; it seemed to go on endlessly in every direction.
She began to get a sense of why the place was so
difficult for Mildred to manage on her own, at age
seventy. As they stopped to let the horses drink from
an irrigation pond, Carrie asked, "Would you really
sell the ranch, Aunt Mildred?"

"I'll try to hang on to it," Mildred answered, "It
doesn't make much money any more, and it's falling
apart, but it's my home. I can't truthfully say that I'd
want to live anywhere else."

"I don't blame you," said Carrie, looking out over
the low, rocky bluffs.

"Where we're standing," Mildred continued, "is
where the first people to live on this land—Native
Americans—lived for thousands of years. Horses have
been galloping across this area since the 1800s."

"Can I gallop with Georgia," Carrie asked. "I've

been wanting to feel what it would be like."

"Go ahead," Mildred said. "Speed is Georgia's middle name. I'll meet you back at the barn. I like to take my time."

Carrie gave Georgia a squeeze with her legs. Georgia immediately broke into a lope.

Carrie put her hand on Georgia's neck. "Come on girl, faster," she whispered. "Let's really run!" She closed her legs tighter against the horse's sides and felt Georgia surge forward. The wind whipped past Carrie's face, bringing tears to her eyes. She could feel the powerful muscle's in Georgia's hindquarters driving them forward while her hooves thundered over the earth, faster and faster until it felt almost as if they were flying.

Carrie's new straw hat blew off her head, but she didn't even notice. She had entered that glorious state where horse and rider felt like one being.

Back at the corral, free of bridle and saddle, Georgia rolled in the dirt to let her body cool down. She had had quite a workout. Carrie walked in circles, stretching out the tight muscles in her calves and thighs.

"That was fun!" Carrie said, as Mildred arrived leading Casey with one hand and holding Carrie's hat in the other.

"You looked like a natural," Mildred said. "You have a lot of skill. I do declare you might just become a western rider after all."

Carrie was flattered by her aunt's praise. But she shared the credit with Georgia. "She's so fast," Carrie said. "She heard me say faster, and we went faster!"

Carrie put her arms around Georgia and whispered, "Thanks for the ride. Tomorrow, more barrels!"

CHAPTER SIX

Becoming a Competitor

As the weeks flew by, Carrie settled into a daily routine of working the barrels with Georgia. Each morning, after finishing her cleaning and grooming chores, Carrie would bring Georgia out to the corral. Mildred would join them, sitting on the fence and calling out advice.

The team could now take the barrels at a lope. "Go! Go home!" Carrie would urge, as they headed for the finish line, which Mildred had marked with bright orange plastic cones. Each time they crossed the finish line, Carrie's heart pounded with excitement. In these moments, Georgia seemed to come fully alive, zooming toward the end with every muscle straining.

"You're becoming quite a team," Mildred called out. "It's a pretty sight to see, the two of you. You've really learned to match Georgia's speed to the finish."

Carrie flushed with pride at her aunt's words. "You're the best horse in the whole world," she whispered to Georgia, stroking her neck. The Paint responded with a proud shake of her brown and white head.

Their practice sessions were hard work, too. Sweat poured from Carrie's face and neck, and dust coated her skin and clothes. Sometimes the lessons left Carrie feeling clumsy and frustrated. Sometimes Georgia grew bored of the training and let Carrie know by anticipating her moves before Carrie signaled with her legs or reins.

"Now you have to learn to rate," Mildred told Carrie.

"What does that mean?" Carrie asked, her voice weary.

"It means getting Georgia to shorten or adjust her stride to make the turn."

Mildred had Carrie walk Georgia to the barrel, then stop, then turn. Walk, stop, turn—over and over and over. She showed Carrie how to sit deep in the saddle and how to use the spoken signal of "whoa" to control Georgia's speed. The walking and stopping and turning and talking were making Carrie dizzy.

"I can't do this!" she cried out. "It feels like I take one step forward and two steps back!"

"You look frustrated," Mildred said.

Carrie put her hand to her face, which was pulled into a stiff frown. "I am," she said. "I'm giving myself a headache, trying so hard."

"I think you're giving your horse a headache, too," Mildred said, pointing at Georgia, who was nosing the ground. "Why don't we stop for today?"

Carrie dismounted and brushed herself off. "Maybe you're right," she said, close to tears. "Maybe we should stop." She led Georgia around the corral to cool her down.

"There comes a time during training," Mildred said gently, "when both horse and rider need to take a break. If you train too much, one or both of you risk getting hurt."

Carrie patted Georgia. "I couldn't let that happen to you," she told her horse. "I couldn't bear to see you hurt."

"I couldn't bear to see *you* hurt," Mildred responded.

Carrie smiled, pleased to know that her aunt cared.

"I have an idea," Mildred said. "Come back to the

house after you get Georgia cooled off and we'll talk it over."

Carrie took her time grooming Georgia, who was covered in sweat. She gave her a cool bath with the water hose, which Georgia seemed to love. It made Carrie feel good to tend to her horse. She took special care to sponge the dust from Georgia's eyes and nostrils and brush around her face.

"Thanks for being so patient with me, Georgia," Carrie said, as she led the horse out to the pasture for some grazing and rest. Georgia nickered in response, her eyes half-closed and her strong body relaxing in the sun.

Carrie found Mildred setting up an old painting easel near the south window of the living room. She was spreading out brushes and paints on the coffee table.

"What are you doing?" Carrie asked. "Are you going to paint?"

"No. You are."

"Me?" said Carrie. Her voice was filled with doubt.

"You see anyone else in the room?" Mildred joked.

"But I don't know how to paint. I'm not an artist."

"Everyone can paint," Mildred said. "If you have eyes and you can see, then you can paint."

"But why?" Carrie asked. "I thought you wanted

to talk about how my training was going."

"I do," said Mildred. "I decided this morning that you need a break from horses. You need to do something else for a while. That way, when you go back to New York next month you can say you learned barrel racing *and* something about painting, too."

Strangely, the thought of returning to New York made Carrie feel sad. She missed her parents a great deal, of course, but her life on the ranch with Mildred and Georgia was so different and special. Carrie liked the easy way she and her aunt went about their days—riding, cooking, doing chores, reading in the evenings, and watching the stars. She loved her long rides with Georgia across the ranch. She even loved her training sessions.

As Mildred continued to arrange the art supplies she looked at Carrie and said quietly, "I have a challenge to offer you."

"What?" asked Carrie.

"I've been giving this a lot of thought. The regional youth rodeo in Sterling is two weeks away. I thought maybe you'd like to enter the barrels with Georgia."

Carrie caught her breath. "Really?" she asked. "Do you think I could do it?"

"I think with some more hard work you might do very well. You certainly have the spirit for competing. Look how hard you've been training just for the fun of it. With a specific goal in mind, there's no telling what you and Georgia could accomplish."

Carrie joined her aunt at the easel. "But the other kids have been competing their whole lives! Could I compete with them?"

Mildred was always honest so she looked at Carrie and said firmly, "I don't know, Carrie. The only way to find out is to enter the event and give it your best. But remember, you're smart and Georgia's fast. That's a winning combination."

Carrie thought about riding Georgia in a real barrel race. She thought about the crowd watching the two of them as they made their best time around the course. She thought about tipping her hat as she and Georgia won a blue ribbon. She thought about handing the ribbon to Mildred and saying, "This is for you."

"I want to," Carrie said quickly. "I want to try."

"Good for you!" Mildred responded, giving Carrie a hug. "I was pretty certain that the offer of real competition would spark your interest. It's in your blood, don't forget. You're a rodeo gal at heart, just like your old aunt was."

"You still are," Carrie said, pulling away and looking at Mildred.

"Having you here this summer has made me feel that way, honey. It's brought back so many fine memories. Even if I have to sell this place, you've given me back my rodeo memories and that's a wonderful gift."

Carrie vowed to herself that she would make Mildred proud by doing her best at Sterling. I'll find a way for Mildred to keep the Western M, too, she thought. There has to be something I can do.

Mildred interrupted her thoughts by telling Carrie to choose a paintbrush. "We're going to start," she said, "by learning to mix colors. So look outside that window there and tell me what colors you see."

Carrie looked out the window and studied the scenery. "Well, I see those two old willow trees on either side of the driveway," Carrie said. "The trunks are brown and the leaves are green."

"What color green?" Mildred asked.

"Um, sort of a dusty green," Carrie said, looking hard at the trees.

"Dusty?"

"Well, more like frosted. Frosted with white."

"Good," said Mildred. "So let's begin by adding some white to the green to match our shade."

Mildred and Carrie spent several happy hours painting the willow trees outside the window. Though Carrie enjoyed it, her mind kept wandering to Georgia, who was probably resting in the sun. She couldn't wait to tell her the wonderful news that the two of them were entering the youth competition in Sterling.

We're going to be a real team, Carrie imagined telling Georgia. We're going to show everyone that we're rodeo people. It's in our blood!

CHAPTER SEVEN

The Storm

"Go, Georgia! To the finish," Carrie urged as they rounded the third barrel and headed to the cone markers.

Mildred, with a stopwatch in her hand, clocked the time as the team sped by her.

"Great!" she called to Carrie. "Your time is getting better and better."

Carrie walked Georgia over to her aunt and dismounted. "What was the time?" she asked nervously.

"Twenty-nine seconds," Mildred answered. "That's a second faster than yesterday. The high twenties are good for a young competitor."

"It's strange how one second can make such a difference," Carrie said. "It doesn't feel any faster."

"In professional barrel racing, a one-hundredth of a second can make the difference between first and second place," Mildred said. "The electronic timers they use nowadays are pretty amazing."

"I can't even imagine a one-hundredth of a second," Carrie said. She pulled a carrot out of her shirt pocket and gave it to Georgia. "Here you go," she said, as the horse happily crunched the snack. "You deserve a treat for all your hard work."

"I think that horse just ate a whole carrot in a one-hundredth of a second," Mildred said.

"Too bad they don't give blue ribbons for eating," Carrie agreed. "Georgia would be a champion."

"Well," said Mildred, "you're making progress. You're shaving seconds from your time, and you rarely knock over a barrel. You should be proud."

"Is my time good enough to win? Or at least not to be embarrassing?"

"Why would you ever be embarrassed for trying? I'll be proud of you if you place last. You and Georgia will always be winners in my book."

"Thanks," Carrie replied. She appreciated her aunt's words. But she wanted more than anything to win a ribbon. And time was running out. There were fewer than two weeks until the youth competition in Sterling. Every day counted. Every practice session was important. And there was so much to remember!

As if she could read Carrie's thoughts, Georgia nuzzled her from behind. Carrie turned around and smiled. Georgia's expression was steady and calm. "What are you trying to tell me?" Carrie asked. "That you're not worried?"

Georgia nickered in response. Carrie sometimes wished Georgia could talk. Then she could ask her, "How do you think we'll do in Sterling? Are you feeling confident? Is there anything you think we should work harder on?"

As it was, Carrie had to rely on Georgia's speed and agility and her own limited "horse smarts" to do well at the rodeo. And we will do well, she promised herself. We will.

Carrie looked up, realizing the sun had

disappeared. To the west and north, the sky was turning almost black with heavy, dark rain clouds. Suddenly the wind kicked up. Fast moving storms had cut Carrie's training sessions short for the past three afternoons in a row.

"It looks like it's going to rain again," Carrie said, pointing to the threatening clouds.

Mildred looked up and gasped. "Goodness!" she exclaimed. "That's not a pretty sight." As she spoke, the wind seemed to double its speed. Dirt blew in their faces, and dried weeds scuttled across the corral.

"What's going on?" Carrie shouted to her aunt, who was studying the sky. The wind was howling now, and Carrie had to hold her hat down with her hand. Raindrops pelted her face.

"Grab Georgia's reins," Mildred shouted back. "Hold her steady."

Carrie hurried over to her horse, who was dancing in circles. Georgia's ears flicked in one direction and then another, as if she were trying to hear a particular sound. "Easy, girl . . . easy," Carrie said, taking the reins. "It's just another storm."

But Georgia was clearly nervous. The noise from the wind was like a shriek, and the blowing dirt hit them from all sides.

Mildred joined them, talking in a low voice. "I don't want you to panic, but I think this might be a pretty bad storm. We need to let Georgia out to pasture with the other horses."

"Why?" Carrie asked. Usually they just took the animals to the barn until a storm passed.

"Because, honey, the barn is up on a rise. If this wind gets worse, the horses could be in danger in the barn. It could fall apart over their heads."

"Will they be safe outside?"

"Horses have instincts. They'll know to get to a low area and wait out the storm. Better get going."

Quickly, Carrie took off Georgia's saddle and bridle and led her to the gate, trying not to be afraid. But she'd never seen her aunt act that way before—businesslike, quiet, and very serious.

Out in the pasture, the other horses stood in a group, whinnying to one another. The rain fell harder, accompanied by crackling thunder and lightning.

Carrie tried her best to comfort Georgia. "It'll be okay," she said. "It'll pass over soon, and we'll go back to our practice." Carrie opened the pasture gate and Georgia jogged out to join the other horses.

Mildred ran quickly to shut the barn doors and cover the two windows with their hinged shutters. "Hurry!" she called to Carrie. Carrie didn't want to

leave Georgia. She wanted to go out to the pasture and stand beside her, her arms safely around Georgia's neck.

"We have to get to the storm shelter," Mildred said, grabbing Carrie's hand. "Now! That's a twister coming!"

The wind lashed them with grit and tumbleweeds. Carrie was sure she could hear the horses calling. Tears stung her eyes and her heart was racing. She was too frightened to look up into the sky and see the twister.

Mildred pulled open the heavy wooden door of the storm shelter and gave Carrie a gentle push toward the cement steps leading down underground. Carrie stopped and looked back at the pasture. "What about the horses?" she cried.

"Don't think about them," commanded Mildred. "Go!" Carrie hurried down the steps into the musty darkness, feeling her way with her hands. It was cool and smelled of earth. Carrie hunched down and pulled her knees to her chest.

Soon Carrie heard the door of the cellar slam shut, and Mildred inched her way in the darkness. She knelt next to Carrie and held her tight. Once her aunt's arms were around her, Carrie bowed her head and sobbed.

"Will the horses die?" Carrie asked, choking on her words.

"Shhh," her aunt soothed, as though Carrie was a small child. "Shhh. The horses will be fine. Everything's going to be fine."

Everything didn't *sound* fine, though. The cellar door rumbled and the wind screamed. The ground above them seemed to shake. The noise was like a freight train, roaring inches above Carrie's head. Carrie snapped a hand over her own mouth, to keep herself from screaming, too.

"I've never been this scared!" she shouted to her aunt, huddling closer.

"The twister's passing through!" Mildred yelled, fighting to be heard over the noise. "It'll be over soon!"

Something big landed on the heavy door above their heads, splitting the wood and tearing at the latch that held it closed.

Carrie screamed in terror, but the sound was lost in the fury of the storm. She ducked her head, whispering, "Please don't let us be swept away."

Surveying the Damage

W hen the wind had at last died down, Mildred said, "I think the worst is over." She squeezed Carrie's hand. "But we'll stay put for a few more minutes."

Carrie straightened from her scrunched–over position on the dirt floor and wiped her eyes. They hadn't been swept away, after all! They were alive and breathing! But everything was strangely still.

"It's so quiet," Carrie whispered. "I don't hear the horses. Do you think that's a bad sign?"

"I don't know," Mildred answered. "You stay here while I take a peek."

Mildred slowly pushed open the splintered shelter

door. Daylight poured into the dirt cellar. Carrie squeezed her eyes shut against the brightness.

"Oh, my!" Mildred said softly, opening the door all the way. Her body seemed to sag a few inches as she looked around.

"Is it bad?" Carrie asked. She moved up the steps behind her aunt.

"Oh, my!" is all Mildred could seem to say. She stepped out of the storm shelter, with Carrie right behind her.

The world outside was eerie. The dark clouds had moved further east and the wind had stopped completely. The damage left behind by the twister was quickly visible, though.

Mildred's red pickup truck was lying upside down on its roof, and the vegetable garden was ruined. A portion of the roof of the house was gone, leaving a gaping hole right where Carrie and Mildred slept.

"The house!" Carrie said, pointing at the torn roof.

"Look at the barn," Mildred said, pointing in the opposite direction.

Carrie whipped around, expecting the worst. But the barn was still standing. And Carrie could see Georgia's bridle draped over the corral fence where she had left it.

"I'm going to check the horses," Carrie said, running towards the gate. Please be okay, Georgia, Carrie prayed silently. I couldn't bear it if anything happened to you!

Out of breath, Carrie kept running. The horses were nowhere to be seen. Finally, she spotted them drinking water from the irrigation ditch. "You're safe!" she shouted, catching sight of Georgia. Counting quickly, she realized that Casey and the other horses were all there. Carrie ran to Georgia and buried her face in the horse's mane. Georgia whinnied and craned her neck toward Carrie.

"Oh, Georgia! Aunt Mildred was right. You *did* find a low spot!"

Georgia seemed calm at that moment, but Carrie didn't want to think about how frightened the horses must have been when the twister thundered past them. She was grateful that she and Mildred and the animals had been spared by the twister.

"I'll be back," Carrie told Georgia. "I have to find Aunt Mildred and try to help her."

Carrie sprinted back and found Mildred standing motionless right where she had left her.

"Are you all right?" Carrie asked, wondering if her aunt was ill or in shock.

"I think so," Mildred finally answered. "I just can't

get up the gumption to go inside and see about the damage."

"I'll go with you," Carrie said. "We'll do it together and it won't seem so scary."

Mildred let Carrie take her hand. Together the two entered the house through the back screen door. The kitchen itself was in one piece, except that the wind through the open door had blown things all over. The floor was scattered with papers, broken cups, tipped-over chairs, and a spilled garbage can.

"The kitchen survived," Carrie said, trying to sound cheerful. She picked up the chairs and righted the garbage. Mildred didn't say a word.

The dining room and living room were also largely untouched. The easel still held a painting of Casey that Mildred had been working on that very morning. Ashes from the fireplace coated the woven Native American rug, but not even a vase or framed picture was broken. Mildred moved to her easel and let out a long sigh.

"Casey's okay," Carrie said, gently.

"That's a blessing," Mildred said.

"This part of the house is fine," Carrie said. "Just a lot of dust."

The rest of the house, however, was not fine. The roof over Carrie's room, Mildred's room, and the office had been completely torn away.

Carrie surveyed her room. The bunk bed she slept on was crushed, and the desk was a pile of rubble. Carrie's belongings were scattered everywhere—clothes, books, papers—all the things she had brought with her from New York.

Carrie opened the top drawer of the desk, which was still in one piece, and found her wallet which held the two hundred dollars she hadn't yet spent. I can give Mildred my money, Carrie thought. It's not a lot, but it could help . . . .

"Oh, honey," Mildred said, her voice cracking. "I'm so sorry. All your things."

"It's okay," Carrie said to her. "They're just things. What's important is that *we're* okay and the horses are okay."

Carrie could see that Mildred was crying, and it made her heart ache. All summer her aunt had been a tower of strength and a well of humor and kindness. She had welcomed Carrie to the ranch with open arms and taught her about barrel racing and gardening and painting. She had taught her about the land, and family, and what's carried in the blood from generations past.

Carrie went to Mildred and hugged her. It was time to return some of her aunt's strength and love.

"Think of it this way," Carrie said, pointing up to the sky. "Remember how we like to go outside and look up at the stars when we can't sleep? Well, now we won't even have to leave our rooms. We'll just lie in our beds and watch the Big Dipper."

"Except," said her aunt with a smile, "we don't have beds to sleep in anymore."

Just then they heard the sound of a car outside. They looked out of Carrie's shattered window toward the driveway.

"It's Spencer Wedum, the county deputy," Mildred said. She straightened her shirt and pushed some stray hair from her face. Carrie thought it was a good sign that Mildred was "sprucing up for company."

Outside, Mildred shook hands with the deputy and introduced Carrie to Spencer.

"You gals okay?" he asked, peering at them closely.

"We're fine," Mildred answered. "The horses are fine. But the house is, well . . ." Mildred pointed at the missing roof.

Spencer sighed and shook his head. He dug the toe of his cowboy boot into the dirt, moving it back and forth. "I'm sure sorry," he said, taking off his hat. "It's a shame what these storms do. Not much warning on this one, either. It came out of nowhere."

"Lucky we were outside and saw it coming," Mildred said. "We had enough time to get to the shelter."

"Anything I can do?" Spencer asked. "I doubt you have phone service. You want me to call anyone?"

"Well," said Mildred, thinking. "My insurance agent, I guess. I'll get her card."

Spencer looked relieved. "You're covered for the damages, then?"

"I don't know, to tell you the truth," Mildred admitted. "It's a pretty old policy."

"How about a place to stay?" the deputy asked. "You can come over to our place, you know. We have plenty of room, and—"

Mildred cut him off with a polite wave of her hand. "We'll be fine, thank you. The kitchen is fine, and my niece and I were just talking about how fun it would be to sleep under the stars." Mildred gave Carrie a wink. "If you wait here, I'll go get that insurance card."

After Mildred left, Carrie moved toward Spencer. "What will happen if she doesn't have the money to make the repairs and the insurance isn't enough?" she asked.

Spencer dug his toe into the ground again. "Well," he said, "it's a shame, but sometimes when a person is your aunt's age and something like this happens, well, that person sometimes has to sell the land and move to someplace more . . . manageable."

"What about the horses?" Carrie asked. "Would they have to be sold, too?"

"I reckon so," he said. "Around here, there's always a market for good, healthy horses."

Carrie felt a burning in her throat and a tight knot in her stomach. She saw her aunt coming out of the door. Be strong, she thought. Aunt Mildred needs your help more than ever.

Carrie didn't have a clue what to do first. How could she find an answer to problems as big as the ones Mildred faced? She thought about calling her parents, but realized it was the middle of the night in Europe. And, besides, what could they do from so far away?

"It's up to me," Carrie said very quietly. "It's up to me."

"Did you say something, honey?" Mildred asked, joining her by the deputy's car.

"Um," Carrie stumbled, "well, I was just saying how it's almost dinner time and I thought I'd go see what I could scrounge up in the kitchen."

Carrie turned and ran back to the house, so that no one could ask her another question. Before she opened the kitchen door, she heard her aunt tell Spencer, "That's one strong young lady, if I say so myself. If it hadn't been for her, I'd still be standing over by the storm shelter with my jaw hanging open."

Carrie smiled and went inside to fix her first dinner.

CHAPTER NINE

Worst Fears

The next day when the insurance adjuster pulled up in her shiny white car, Carrie fled to the barn. She didn't want to be in the house while a complete stranger poked around and wrote notes about the storm damage on her official clipboard.

All morning Carrie and Mildred had worked around the house, doing what repairs they could. Warren and Daniel had come over before sunrise with freshly baked cinnamon rolls made by Warren's wife. They helped nail boards across the broken windows, and hitched the rake to the tractor to clean up debris around the property. They even righted Mildred's truck.

It was hot—in the high eighties already—and

Carrie felt sweaty and dirty. She hadn't been able to take a shower yet because of the damage to the bathroom, but seeing Georgia gave her an instant boost.

"Hi, girl!" Carrie said, opening the door to her stall. Georgia was glad to see her, nickering and flicking her dark tail.

"Let's take you outside," Carrie said. "You could use some fresh air and exercise."

Out in the corral, Carrie noticed that all three barrels were lying on their sides and scattered in every direction. She didn't have the heart to set them straight. In fact, she decided she didn't have the heart to even stay inside the corral. The thought of racing around barrels seemed trivial, in light of the problems on the Western M.

"I guess the rodeo doesn't matter much, now," Carrie said to Georgia. "What matters is helping Aunt Mildred and finding a way to save the ranch. And save . . . you," Carrie finished softly, mounting Georgia.

Carrie decided to take Georgia out for a fast ride to the bluffs and back. "That will make us feel better," she said, nudging her horse to the gate. Carrie wanted to gallop fast and think of nothing but the sound of Georgia's hooves beating the ground and the breeze blowing on her face.

Georgia had a different idea. Very slowly, but with great purpose, the horse turned and walked toward one of the tipped barrels. She bent her head to the ground and nosed the barrel. She shifted her weight from back legs to front and let out a loud whinny.

"What are you doing?" Carrie asked, feeling impatient. "Let's go!"

Again, Georgia nudged the barrel and whinnied.

"What do you want?" demanded Carrie. "What is it?"

"She wants to work the barrels, just like every other day," said Mildred, who was approaching.

"Aunt Mildred, I didn't see you," Carrie said. "I thought you were still at the house."

"Well, it didn't take that city gal too long to do her figuring," Mildred said. "In any case, she's gone now. You ought to think about putting your horse through her paces."

"What did she say?" Carrie asked, trying to keep her voice steady and casual.

Mildred, like Carrie, looked as if she could use a long, hot bath and about a week's worth of sleep. "Oh, not much," she replied, giving Carrie a feeble smile.

"Please tell me what she said," Carrie asked again.

"There you go, being stubborn again." Mildred tried to laugh, but the noise she made came out sounding like a cry.

"Will the insurance be enough?"

Her aunt paused before answering. "Just barely. Enough for a new roof. Honey, there's no easy way to say this, I'm going to have to sell the place."

"No!" yelled Carrie. She startled Georgia, who jumped at the sudden, loud sound.

"It breaks my heart, too, Carrie. But I don't have the strength nor the extra money to rebuild the ranch and then keep it going. I don't see any other choice."

"What about . . . what about the horses?" Carrie whispered, trying not to scare Georgia again. But Georgia stood perfectly still, as though she were waiting to hear the answer, too.

"I can't keep horses if I don't have land," Mildred said sadly. "I'll have to sell them."

"Even Georgia?" Carrie asked. She couldn't bear to think of Georgia having to leave the only home she'd ever known to go with strangers who might not care that she was bred to be a champion barrel racer. Her heart pounded in her chest as she waited for her aunt to answer.

"Even Georgia."

Carrie felt dizzy. She thought if she didn't get off

Georgia that very moment, she might fall off. Her stomach heaved, and she was afraid she was about to be sick. Carrie dismounted and went to lean against the fence.

"Are you okay?" Mildred asked. "You'd better sit down."

Carrie sat in the dirt and held her head in her hands. She had been trying so hard to be strong for her aunt. Before she had had hope that everything might turn out all right, that the storm damage could be fixed, and life would go on just as it had all summer. Now, it was official. Mildred would have to sell the ranch. And the horses. Carrie might never see Georgia again.

"Is there anything I can do?" Carrie asked. "What if I call my parents and ask them . . ."

"Carrie," her aunt interrupted, "it's a nice thought. But your folks don't have the kind of money it would take to maintain the ranch, and they're not ranch folks, honey. They're city folks. They like their life."

"But . . ."

"No buts," said Mildred gently. "There comes a time when you have to face reality and be graceful about it. I've had a wonderful life here. Better than most. I've been blessed with all these years on the land, my years with your uncle Donald, my horses, my

rodeo days. And I've been blessed with having you with me this summer."

"But where will you go?" Carrie asked, wiping her nose. "Where will you live?"

"In Yuma, I suppose," Mildred said. "Closer to folks. You know, I do get lonely out here from time to time."

"You could come live with us," Carrie said, brightening at the thought.

"Well, that's the nicest offer I've had in a long time," Mildred said. "But you know me, Carrie. After a week in the city I just get itchy and cranky and I want to see the stars."

"What can I do?" Carrie asked helplessly.

"You can get up on that horse and get to work, that's what you can do. The rodeo is next week and we have a load of work to do."

"Maybe tomorrow," Carrie said.

Georgia moved closer to Carrie. She leaned her head down and pushed Carrie's shoulder.

"Go away," Carrie mumbled.

Mildred put her hands on her hips and cleared her throat. "Maybe I haven't made myself clear," she said. "We have work to do. We need to get a couple seconds off your time if you don't want the local gals to whip the saddle blanket off you."

"Who's being stubborn, now?" Carrie asked, standing up.

"You ain't seen nothin' yet!" Mildred joked.

Carrie gave her aunt a mock salute and helped Mildred set the barrels up and put them in the proper formation. The orange plastic cones were nowhere to be seen. "Probably blown to the edges of the earth," Mildred said, drawing a line in the dirt with her foot. "Here's your finish line."

Carrie walked Georgia through the cloverleaf pattern several times. When they began to jog, though, Georgia knocked over the last two barrels.

"See?" Carrie said. "I'm tired and so is Georgia."

"There's nothing wrong with Georgia," Mildred said, shaking her head. "You've lost your spirit. You have to bring out the best in your horse, honey. If you don't care enough to win, then Georgia won't care either."

"But I *don't* care anymore!" Carrie exclaimed. "How can I care about the Sterling rodeo when you're going to lose the ranch and I'll never see Georgia again? What's the point?"

"The point is," Mildred said, "that it's important to finish things that you start. I know you can do it. And nothing would make me happier than to end this chapter of my life with a spirit of celebration."

Carrie knew in her heart that Mildred was right. It would be foolish to quit now, after they had worked so hard. She took a long breath, nodded, and sat deep into the saddle. Mildred set her stopwatch and signaled Carrie to begin.

"Let's go, girl," Carrie said to Georgia, and they began the course. Carrie concentrated on all the elements: making the pocket, scissoring her legs on the turns, using her legs and reins to guide Georgia. They made every turn this time, and as they galloped to the finish, Carrie knew it was their best ride ever.

"Yes!" shouted Mildred, clicking off the stopwatch. "That's the way to go! That's the way to ride! It's your best time yet!"

Carrie leaned forward, hugging Georgia's neck. "You're amazing," she said. "You just know what to do."

Mildred, with her first real smile of the day, went to get some cold drinks and see if the telephone line had been repaired.

Carrie sat on the fence, allowing Georgia to cool down. She reached into her pocket for the end–of–session carrot she always brought.

As Georgia crunched happily, Carrie suddenly had an idea. "Hey," she said to Georgia, fingering her tousled mane, "I've got it! A celebration! Aunt Mildred said she'd like nothing better than to end with a big celebration. What if we plan the biggest party in the world for her? We could . . . we could call some of Mildred's old rodeo friends to come to the Western M for a real farewell party. I still have my money from Mom and Dad . . . we could . . . oh, my gosh, there's so much to do! What do you think, girl?"

Georgia swallowed her carrot and threw her head up and down, looking for all the world like she was nodding in agreement.

"Leave it all to me," Carrie whispered. "Just don't tell anyone. It has to be a surprise."

CHAPTER TEN

Finishing Touches

"What are you doing?" Mildred asked Carrie the following morning.

Carrie quickly shut the scrapbook she was looking at. "Oh, nothing," she said. "Just taking a break from cleaning."

In truth, Carrie was making a list of her aunt's rodeo friends and looking for any clues about phone numbers and home towns. If she was going to surprise Aunt Mildred with a party, there was so much to be done.

"Do you want to drive into Yuma with me?" Mildred asked. "I'm tired of cleaning up after that storm, and I thought a drive might do us some good.

We need groceries, and I have to price bathroom tile."

"I'd love to," Carrie answered. "I need a new shirt for the rodeo. Something bright to bring me good luck."

What Carrie really wanted to do was start making phone calls to Mildred's friends. The ranch was still without phone service, so maybe the telephone company in Yuma could help her.

Carrie went to find her wallet with the two hundred dollars. She'd need to pay for the long distance calls and arrange for some food for the party. She hoped her aunt's errands in town would take enough time for Carrie to do her own errands.

In the car, Carrie gazed out the window. She still couldn't believe that she was spending her last week and a half at the ranch, and that she would never be able to come back again. The thought of saying good-bye to Georgia forever made Carrie sadder than she had ever been in her life. Each day when they practiced, Carrie stared at Georgia, trying to remember every detail of her beloved horse.

Every time they rounded a barrel, Carrie would try to memorize the feel of Georgia's strong muscles and fast legs. Aunt Mildred had told Carrie about a camp in Nevada that taught barrel racing. She'd sent for the brochure, hoping to keep Carrie interested in the sport.

"You can go there next summer," Mildred had said. "I'm sure your parents would consider sending you."

"It wouldn't be the same," Carrie had told her.

In Yuma, they agreed to meet back at the car in an hour and a half. Carrie checked her watch and sped off to Norman's to buy the first inexpensive shirt she could find. Mildred went to the hardware store to price bathroom tile.

After paying for a yellow shirt with black stitching, Carrie went to the telephone building. "I hope you can help me," she told the woman at the front desk. "I'm on a secret mission to plan a party for my aunt Mildred who is selling the Western M."

The woman looked surprised, then truly sad. "Oh, dear," she said to Carrie. "I sure am sorry to hear that. Your aunt is a wonderful lady. The whole town thinks the world of her. We claim her as our very own rodeo legend."

Glad to have someone on her side, Carrie explained her plan and showed the woman her list of names. "I want to pay cash for the calls," she said. "I don't want my aunt to know anything."

To Carrie's great surprise, she and the operator were able to locate seven of the twelve women from the rodeo circuit. Three lived in Colorado, two in Texas, one in California, and one in Montana. Each one said she would do her best to come to the party.

Carrie looked at her watch. An hour had quickly disappeared. "Thank you so much!" Carrie said to the operator. "I can't believe it was that easy."

"Oh, the wonders of modern technology," the woman said with a laugh. "Glad to help. If I can help with anything else, you just give me a call. My name's Brenda and I'm here every day except Sunday."

Then Carrie remembered the food! You couldn't have a party without food. She took a handful of quarters and the phone book and sat down again. To her surprise, the Yuma phone book had no listings under caterers, party planners, or chefs.

"If this were New York," Carrie told Brenda, "there would be three hundred caterers to choose from!"

Brenda nodded and laughed. "I'm sure that's true," she said. "Folks in small towns either go to the city for what they need or go without."

"Denver!" cried Carrie. "That's it! I'll call Denver."

She quickly flipped open the Denver phone book. There were over twenty caterers listed. Carrie dropped a quarter into the pay phone and made her first call. But her excitement quickly vanished. The first caterer wouldn't deliver all the way to Yuma. The second would come but wanted four hundred dollars. The third call was answered by someone who told Carrie he didn't do business with children.

"Children," Carrie muttered. "Four hundred dollars." She put her head down on her arms and sighed.

"Why not try a potluck," Brenda suggested. "Everyone could bring a dish to share."

"I want it to be a real party, with special food already prepared," Carrie replied. "I don't want Mildred's guests to have to bring anything."

With a sinking feeling, Carrie thanked Brenda for her help and walked outside. She still had twenty minutes before she had to meet Mildred. As she passed the Broken Wheel Cafe, she decided to cheer herself up with a chocolate shake and onion rings.

The restaurant was empty except for two teenage boys eating a huge plate of french fries with ketchup, and Frankie, the owner, who was listening to the radio and doing the crossword puzzle.

Carrie slipped into a booth and took a deep breath. She only had seventeen minutes left. "What am I going to do?" she said out loud.

"Do about what?" Frankie asked, smiling down at Carrie.

Carrie looked up, startled. "Oh, hi," she said. "You surprised me."

Frankie sat down across from her. "Why the long

face?" she asked. "Whatever it is, it can't be that bad."

"It is," Carrie answered. "I'm planning a party for Aunt Mildred before she sells the ranch. Things were going pretty well until I called some caterers in Denver. One wanted four hundred dollars for some stuffed peppers and a fruit plate, and another refused to do business with a child."

Frankie laughed and pulled at her long white ponytail. "Talk about big city prices and big city attitude! Listen, honey, here's an idea. I would never call myself a fancy thing like a caterer, but I do serve up a pretty terrific barbecue with all the fixings."

"That's perfect!" Carrie said, almost jumping out of her seat. "But I only have a hundred and sixty dollars left."

"What a coincidence," said Frankie. "That's precisely how much I charge."

Carrie explained her plan to Frankie, who wrote a few notes on a paper napkin. They worked out the menu and decided that Frankie would arrive at the Western M at noon the following Saturday to set up and cook, while Carrie and Mildred were at the Sterling rodeo. When they returned, the guests would be there, the ribs would be smoking, and the party would be ready to begin.

Frankie promised to keep everything a secret.

Then Carrie paid Frankie for the barbecue with her wad of cash, proud of herself for all that she'd accomplished.

"If I can be of any more help at all," Frankie said, "you just give me a call. I'd do anything to help Mildred. She's a peach. I can't believe she's selling her place, but then again, I can't imagine how she's kept it going all these years."

"There is one thing you can do," Carrie said, right before she left. "You can spread the word here in town, and invite my aunt's friends to the party. I want it to be a great send-off."

"You can count on me," Frankie said, making some more notes on her napkin.

When Carrie and Mildred got back to the ranch, the construction crew was finishing for the day. The new roof was completed and the outside looked almost as good as new. There was still a lot to be done inside, but the county inspector had come by to say that the house was safe and sound.

Carrie looked at her watch. There was still time to work with Georgia. Every day counted, because the rodeo was less than a week away. "Want to time me on the barrels?" Carrie asked. Mildred agreed, and went inside to get her stopwatch. By the time she returned to the corral, Carrie and Georgia were making their practice runs.

"Ready?" Mildred asked, finding a seat on the fence.

"Ready," Carrie answered. She and Georgia started well, heading for the first barrel. They picked up speed as they neared the second, but knocked it over on the turn. The third turn was nearly perfect and Georgia gave it her all to the finish.

"Twenty-eight," Mildred shouted, clicking off the watch. "You've done twenty-eight seconds with no mistakes before. If you can do that in Sterling, you can place in the top ten."

Carrie smiled, but she wondered if she and Georgia could run a flawless race with all the added pressure of a real competition. What if the crowd and the announcers and the newness of everything made Carrie so nervous she couldn't communicate with her horse?

That night, lying in her newly repaired bunk bed, Carrie couldn't sleep. Pictures flashed through her overtired brain: rodeos, parties, storm damage, the Western M, her parents, returning to New York, and, of course, Georgia.

Suddenly, Carrie sat up in bed. She wanted to talk to Georgia. After all, Georgia was her partner.

In the barn, Georgia was lying in the soft straw, relaxed and sleeping. Carrie watched for a few minutes, as the horse's sides moved in and out with rhythmic breathing.

"Hey, girl," Carrie whispered. "I hate to wake you, but I have to talk to you."

Georgia stirred, and then quickly rose.

Carrie opened the door to the stall and stood next to Georgia, stroking her neck. "How are you?" she asked.

Georgia shook her head and snorted.

"I've been thinking about the rodeo," Carrie said softly. "I can't get to sleep. How can you sleep so easily?"

Turning away from Carrie, Georgia took a drink of water.

"I've been worrying about knocking over barrels and disappointing Mildred. And disappointing you, after all our hard work. Do you think everything's going to be okay?"

Georgia turned around and nickered, looking at Carrie. Carrie looked back, wishing she could know what went on inside Georgia's mind on a moonlit night, but she felt strangely reassured, just being near her horse. When she was with Georgia, she always had the feeling that things would be fine.

After a while, Carrie said good night to Georgia and went to look for the Big Dipper.

Rodeo Day

Carrie's big day finally arrived. It was Saturday, August 17 and the Sterling Youth Competition Rodeo was about to begin. Carrie and Georgia had just finished their practice round and were watching the other girls warm up inside the ring.

"They all look so good," Carrie said with awe.

"You'll do fine," Mildred said encouragingly.

"These girls are the best from the region."

"And you," said Mildred, "are the best from the Western M. Just stay focused on your task and don't get distracted by the other girls."

"I'm number six out of fifteen," Carrie noted, looking at the program in her hand.

"That's good," said Mildred, "just about the middle. You should watch the riders before you and after. Study what they do with their bodies and with their horses."

"My stomach is doing flip–flops," Carrie groaned.

"Watch this rider," said Mildred, pointing to a red–headed girl in a plaid shirt. "See how she sits down in the saddle as she goes to the first turn? Now she's scissoring her legs on the back of the turn. Her head and upper body are aimed directly at her point for the second barrel."

"She's great," Carrie agreed. "It says on the program her horse is named Lincoln."

"Don't forget to pick your point for the first barrel," Mildred continued. "That's very important. When you cross the finish, ease Georgia to a stop instead of just skidding. I've seen riders stop too soon, before they'd even crossed the finish line."

Mildred's advice helped Carrie to concentrate on her goal, instead of on the arena, which was filling up with people. The only audience Carrie had ever performed for was Mildred, and sometimes Warren and Daniel. It would be strange to have so many people watching.

Mildred looked at her watch and said, "Oh, my. You should be getting back to Georgia. I think they're about to get started. Be sure to check her feet, and recheck your saddle."

"Okay," Carrie said, trying to smile at her aunt. "Thanks for everything."

Mildred reached into her pocket and handed Carrie a faded blue ribbon. Carrie could barely make out the lettering. First Place, 1959. Amarillo, Texas, she read silently.

"Was this yours?" Carrie asked.

"Yes, missy. It's for good luck. I wanted you to have a blue ribbon before the race so you'd know that no matter how you do today, you're first place in my book."

"Oh, Aunt Mildred, you're the best!" cried Carrie. She tucked the ribbon into the pocket of her new yellow shirt, thinking how the faded blue of the ribbon exactly matched the color of the evening sky at the Western M.

"Have fun!" Mildred shouted, as Carrie hurried away.

As Mildred went to find her seat in the bleachers, Carrie went behind the gates to be with Georgia. Georgia seemed calm, as usual, and patiently stood while Carrie rechecked her equipment. Carrie also checked Georgia's legs for bruises and her hooves for stones. Everything was fine. Georgia looked beautiful. A true, proud Paint with the prettiest coat and fastest legs in Colorado.

Carrie took out the blue ribbon and looked at it. Then she showed it to her horse. "Look, Georgia. We already have a blue ribbon, so we just need to have a good time, okay?"

Georgia nickered and flicked her tail.

"Let's show them what we can do," Carrie whispered, as the first rider was announced.

Carrie watched the first few riders carefully, noticing their different skills and approaches. When she was two riders away from her start, though, she stopped watching. She closed her eyes, put her hand on Georgia's side, and tried to picture the perfect race.

In her mind, she and Georgia made a terrific run, handling the rate and pocket with ease at each barrel, and galloping aggressively across the finish. A voice interrupted.

"Now, ladies and gentlemen, number six, Miss

Carrie Gordon. This little gal is riding a Paint named Georgia and is representing the Western M Ranch. This is her first competition, and she hails from that famous rodeo town, New York City."

There was a quick rise of friendly laughter at the announcer's remark, but Carrie didn't notice as she positioned Georgia at the starting line. Every muscle in her body was tensed as she waited for the buzzer to sound. "Let's do it!" she whispered to Georgia. Carrie picked her point for the first barrel and willed every cell in her body to pay attention.

The buzzer sounded, high pitched and direct. The electronic timer began flashing its hundredths of seconds. Carrie and Georgia took off for the first barrel. Just as they had practiced hundreds of times, they made a clean, crisp turn. Good job, Carrie thought.

With the second barrel squarely in sight, Carrie scissored her legs. Georgia made a tight arc around the barrel, but just then Carrie felt her left foot slip from the stirrup. Carrie knew she had no time to adjust her foot. She knew she would have to sit deep in the saddle and do the best job ever using her legs and reins. Keep going, keep going, she told herself.

Momentarily distracted by her foot, Carrie let Georgia brush the third barrel. Carrie was sure it

would tumble over and cost her five seconds. But miraculously, the barrel stayed up, and Carrie urged Georgia into a gallop toward the finish.

Carrie didn't even hear the timer as they crossed the finish line. All she heard was the roar of the crowd as her time was displayed on the scoreboard: 26.83 seconds!

Carrie slowed Georgia to a gentle stop, remembering her aunt's words. Only then did she look at her time. "Our best ever!" she cried, hugging Georgia. "Our best ever!"

Carrie was so happy she didn't care whether the time was good enough to place. Filled with joy, Carrie focused on leading Georgia out of the arena and finding her a well-deserved place to rest and drink some water.

Carrie instantly spotted Mildred, who was making her way toward her. "You did it!" Mildred cried. She hugged Carrie and then gave Georgia a loving pat. "That was a sight to behold!"

"Did you see my foot slip?" Carrie asked.

"Yes. I was worried for a minute, there. But you handled it like a pro and just kept going."

"I was worried, too!" Carrie admitted. "Of all the things that could go wrong, that's one I hadn't thought of."

"I'm so proud of you," Mildred said. "You're a fine match, you and Georgia. Just like I've been telling you, it's in your blood . . . both of you."

Suddenly Carrie felt terribly sad. The end of the competition meant the end of everything: summer, training for the barrels, her time with Mildred, her stay on the ranch, and her partnership with Georgia. Tears filled her eyes. Carrie wanted to be alone with Georgia. She wanted to leave the crowded arena and just ride, long and silent.

"Where are you going?" Mildred asked with concern.

"I'm just . . . I'm just going to get Georgia ready to haul back in the trailer."

"Not so fast," Mildred said, putting her hand on Carrie's arm.

"Why?" asked Carrie. "Should I be doing something else?"

"Yes," laughed Mildred. "I'm not one hundred percent sure, but I think you had better get ready to ride Georgia out there into the middle of the ring and accept a ribbon."

Carrie looked at her aunt with suspicion. Surely this couldn't be true? Had her time been good enough to place? With all these talented local girls?

"There's only a few riders left, but if I'm not

mistaken, Miss Carrie Gordon from New York City, you and your Paint have one of the best times so far."

Carrie was stunned. She hadn't been paying attention to the announcer. There was too much going on both around her and inside her head. She leaned against Georgia. "Are you sure?" she asked.

"There are only a few things I'm sure of in this life, honey. One is that you never know when a twister is going to hit, and the other is barrel racing!" Mildred threw back her head and laughed the warm, rich laugh that Carrie had grown to love.

Just then the announcer broke in. "That completes barrel racing, or as we old cowboys call it— chasing cans! After the winners are announced, we'll move on to our calf-roping event. Don't forget to visit the concession stand. The profits today benefit the Sterling 4-H Club. Now for our winning gals: in third place is Linda Anson from Grant, Nebraska. Second place goes to Nancy Horton from our very own Sterling, Colorado. And in first place, newcomer Carrie Gordon, trained by her aunt and our old friend, Mildred Wilson! Carrie, we hope we see you again next year!"

The crowd burst into applause and whistles. Carrie couldn't believe her ears. Mildred practically had to push her up into the saddle. In the center of the ring, flanked by the other two winners and their horses, Carrie thought her heart was going to burst. How she wished her parents could be there to see her accept her blue ribbon! Her friends at home would never believe this!

Carrie waved and smiled at the crowd. When the clapping didn't ease up, she tipped her hat. Georgia, her head held high, was the perfect picture of a champion. Carrie nodded her head as the applause continued, and wiped away tears with the back of her hand.

"This is for you, Aunt Mildred," she said to herself. "And for you, Georgia."

As Carrie guided Georgia out of the ring, she suddenly remembered the party that was being prepared at the Western M. Carrie hoped that Mildred's friends had arrived safely and that the ribs were cooking slowly.

But more than anything, she hoped that Mildred would be surprised and honored by her big farewell to the Western M.

Happy Trails

66 L et's go to a fancy restaurant to celebrate," Mildred said to Carrie on their way home from the rodeo.

"Um, well . . ." Carrie stumbled. She *had* to get Mildred to drive directly back to the ranch. Everyone would be waiting to begin the party. "You know, I'm pretty tired. What I'd really like is to go back home."

Mildred looked at her carefully. "Are you sure?"

"I'm sure." Carrie nodded.

For the rest of the drive, Mildred and Carrie discussed the rodeo. It already felt like a dream to Carrie. She couldn't clearly remember her ride, except for the moment her foot slipped out of the stirrup and the moment she was handed the blue ribbon.

Once they reached sight of the Western M, Carrie saw a line of cars and trucks in the driveway. She looked over at her aunt, who was peering through the windshield.

"Now what do you suppose all those cars are doing in my driveway?" she asked. She sounded concerned. Carrie wanted to ease her mind, but she didn't want to give away the surprise.

"Why don't we go find out?" Carrie urged.

Mildred quickly parked her truck behind the others and headed toward the house. Carrie followed closely, trying not to giggle with excitement. As they rounded the corner at the back of the house, a crowd of people came into view.

A huge paper banner fluttered between two trees. It said, "Farewell to the Western M!" Paper lanterns dangled from the clothesline and balloons floated above the backs of lawn chairs. The barbecue pit sizzled and sent a stream of wood smoke into the air. All around, groups of people talked and laughed, holding paper cups of lemonade.

Someone spotted Mildred and shouted, "She's here! The guest of honor!" Others shouted, "Surprise!" and then began a chorus of "For She's a Jolly Good Fellow."

Mildred gasped and put her hand across her heart. Her jaw dropped and she shook her head slowly, back and forth.

"Well, I'll be!" she finally said. "You nearly gave me a heart attack. What's going on here?"

A woman Mildred's age, wearing a blue cowboy hat and blue denim dress, stepped forward.

"Why it's Delores DeHart!" Mildred said. "I haven't seen you since the dinosaurs roamed the earth!" The two women hugged and laughed, until tears streamed from their eyes.

"How? What?" Mildred sputtered. "How did you all get here?" Mildred looked around at the people gathered in her yard. She saw old rodeo pals, friends from town, neighbors from nearby farms and ranches. She spotted Warren and his wife, Daniel, and Frankie who was overseeing the barbecue pit.

"It was your niece," Delores said. "She planned the whole thing. Called up all your old friends and told them they'd better come by and say goodbye to

the Western M and give you a big send-off."

Mildred looked at Carrie, who smiled back at her. "You did all this?" she asked.

Carrie nodded. "I wanted to do something for you. After all you've done for me. I wanted you not to feel so sad about . . . selling the ranch and the horses."

Mildred put her arms around Carrie. Then she said to the crowd, "For those of you who haven't met her, this is my great-niece, Carrie Gordon, who just happens to have taken first place in the barrels at the Sterling rodeo earlier today. May I present the next generation of champion!"

Everyone clapped and cheered at this news, and Carrie blushed a deep red. She didn't know what to say. Finally, she said, "I have to give credit to Georgia, my Paint. Speaking of Georgia, she's still in the trailer and I should go take care of her."

Carrie left the party, which seemed to be going wonderfully, and went to tend to Georgia. Back in the barn at last, Carrie concentrated on her horse.

"How're you doing?" she said, as she brushed Georgia's coat. "What a day, huh?"

Georgia seemed tired, and Carrie couldn't blame her. They had all been up at dawn to get ready to go to Sterling. "You rest," Carrie told Georgia. "But first I have a treat for you."

Carrie fed Georgia her favorite, carrots, laughing at how quickly the horse swallowed them. "First place in barrels and first place in eating!"

Carrie heard the barn door open and turned to see Mildred. "Hi!" she called. "How's the party?"

"It's terrific," Mildred said. "I'm still pinching myself to make sure it's really happening."

"I'm glad you're enjoying it," Carrie said.

"I can't find the words to thank you, Carrie. It must have been quite a job to pull this off by yourself."

"I had a lot of help," admitted Carrie. "People couldn't have been nicer. You have a lot of friends."

"That I do," Mildred said. "I'm rich in friends and that's a lot."

Carrie cleared her throat and tried to look busy grooming Georgia. "When do you think we'll see each other again?" she asked.

"I've been thinking about that, too," Mildred said. "I'm due for another trip to New York. We could hit the museums and the theater. What do you say?"

"Great," Carrie said, trying to sound cheerful. "Maybe we could rent some horses in Central Park and . . ."

"Knock down some joggers?" Mildred joked.

They laughed, but both of them felt the deep

sadness beneath the laughter.

"I hope Georgia will be happy with her new owners," Carrie said.

Mildred was silent, and Carrie put her face against Georgia's neck, trying to memorize the earthy, animal smell. Soon she would be smelling city smells: smoke, car fumes, street-corner food. Carrie couldn't wait to see her parents, but returning to New York would be a big change after her summer on the Western M.

Then a voice called out, "Can I join in?" Mildred's old friend Delores entered the barn, followed by Roberta and Evelyn, who long ago had helped to start the barrel-racing event. Carrie had seen their pictures many times in Mildred's scrapbooks. Although they were wrinkled now, with gray hair, they still resembled the vigorous young women from the black-and-white photos.

"You're missing your own party," Delores said.

"They're serving up the ribs," added Roberta.

"Someone's passing around your old scrapbooks," Evelyn said.

"I was just on my way," Mildred said, patting Carrie's shoulder. "We're just making a plan to see each other in New York City next summer. You see, we're both a couple of stubborn gals, so neither of us is any good at saying good-bye."

"Why say good-bye?" Delores asked. "Why not say, 'See you next summer on the Western M'?"

"What do you mean?" Mildred asked. "I'm selling the Western M."

"To me," Delores interrupted.

"What!" gasped Carrie, looking up from her horse.

"I've been poking around here since I arrived at noon," explained Delores. "I've been looking for an investment opportunity, and I think the Western M Rodeo School and Stables might be just the thing."

"What are you saying?" Mildred asked.

Delores laughed. "For a fast rider, you catch on slowly. I want to buy the Western M and all the horses. I want you to live here and manage the place, like you always have. I want your help in starting a rodeo school. How else are we going to keep the sport of barrel racing alive? We may be old, but we still have a lot to teach these young gals about 'chasing cans'!"

"That's for sure!" Carrie agreed, barely able to keep from jumping up and down with happiness.

"And Carrie," Delores continued, "you are also part of my plans. We can't let a champion slip away from us. Any chance of you coming out here next summer and helping with the school?"

"Yes!" Carrie shouted. This time she *did* jump up and down. "What about Georgia?"

"Well—," began Delores.

"I love your idea," Mildred said, "but I have one condition. Carrie gets Georgia. Full ownership. They're a team."

"It's a deal," Delores said. "Georgia's a champion, too. She'll be very useful to our school."

Carrie could hardly believe this sudden change in events. The Western M wouldn't be sold to strangers! Mildred would still live here! The women would start a rodeo school! And Georgia was hers!

"I don't think I've ever been this happy," Carrie said, hugging her aunt.

"I owe it all to you," Mildred said. "If you hadn't made all those calls, found my old rodeo pals, and invited them here, well, I'd be packing my bags."

Carrie suddenly had an idea. "We should take a picture of all of you," she said to the women. "Just like in the scrapbook. Sitting on the fence, holding your hats."

"A before and after kind of thing?" Mildred joked.

"No," explained Carrie. "A picture of champions, then and now."

"Well," said Delores, "we need you to be in that picture, too. You're one of us—just a few years younger!"

So the women and Carrie posed on the fence, holding their hats, their hair blowing in the cool evening breeze. Warren snapped several pictures as the women smiled and said "rodeo" instead of "cheese."

Then Carrie slipped down from the fence and whispered to her aunt, "Can I take Georgia out? Just until the sun sets? Then I'll come back and join the party."

"Sure," said Mildred. "You go ahead."

Carrie ran to the barn to tack up. "This is the perfect way to end a perfect day," she told Georgia.

Georgia whinnied as they left the barn, pointing her handsome head into the wind. Carrie mounted and the two took off toward the bluffs. Carrie wanted to see the sunset, which was already turning the sky lovely shades of pink and orange, like one of Mildred's paintings.

As they moved from a lope to a gallop, Carrie felt the wind in her face. She smelled the sage and prairie grass and heard the first of the evening's crickets.

"Paint in the sky," Carrie said, marveling at the colors of the sunset.

"And my very own Paint!" she added, feeling the speed and power of her beloved horse as they raced across the Western M.

FACTS
ABOUT THE BREED

You probably know a lot about Paints from reading this book. Here are some more interesting facts about this bi-colored American breed.

⋂ Paints generally stand between 15 and 16 hands high. Instead of using feet and inches, all horses are measured in hands and inches. A hand is equal to four inches.

⋂ Like the pinto, the Paint is white and black or white and brown. In coloring, a Paint horse is usually a pinto. But unlike the pinto, Paint horses must be the offspring of registered Thoroughbreds, Paints, or Quarter Horses.

∩ Paints have two types of coat pattern—
overo and tobiano. The white splashes on an
overo horse are irregular and do not cross the
horse's back. The overo's legs are usually dark
colored, and the face is often white. The tail of
an overo is usually a solid color.

∩ A tobiano usually has a dark-colored head
with small white markings, such as a star, a
stripe, or a snip. The spots of the coat are
regular and often make the shape of a shield
on the horse's chest. The legs are usually white
below the knees. The tail is often two colors.

∩ The names Paint and pinto come from the
Spanish word *pintado*, which means "painted."
Horses with this coat pattern have also been
called calicos, patches, and Indian ponies. The
Paint of today is descended from the Spanish
horses brought to America in the 16th century.

∩ Paints sometimes have blue or white eyes

instead of brown. In the West, horses with such eyes are known as China-eyed, glass-eyed, walleyed, cotton-eyed, and blue-eyed. If a horse has just one light colored eye, it is called watch-eyed.

∩ The Paint is a stock-type horse. This means that the horse is physically suited for work with livestock. Paints have strong hind quarters and well-muscled legs. They can gallop fast and turn quickly. As a result they excel at barrel racing, roping, and cutting.

∩ The American Paint Horse Association in Fort Worth, Texas, has registered qualified Paint horses since its founding in 1965. In addition to having the right pedigree and meeting the breed's color requirements, a horse must stand over 14 hands high to be registered as a Paint.

∩ Before the formation of Paint horse

societies, many Paints had to go unregistered. Because the American Quarter Horse Association will not register horses with "excessive white" markings despite their bloodlines, Paints were excluded from this registry. In response to this restriction, two groups formed to preserve the Paint horse's heritage—The American Paint Horse Association and the American Paint Stock Horse Association. In 1965 the two groups merged to form the American Paint Horse Association (APHA).

∩ The APHA now has over a quarter of a million horses registered. The Association registers approximately 25,000 new foals a year and has become the third largest registry in terms of the number of new horses registered per year in the United States.

∩ There are American Paint Horse Association regional clubs in Austria, Belgium,

Canada, France, Germany, Italy, Luxembourg, Netherlands, Sweden, and Switzerland, in addition to the many clubs in the United States.

∩ Paints, like their Thoroughbred and Quarter Horse ancestors, are great racers. There are Paint races in Oklahoma, Texas, Idaho, Wyoming, Arizona, and Kansas. Paints are excellent sprinters. They race over distances between 220 and 870 yards, with 350 yards being the most common racing distance.

∩ Every year in July the APHA holds its World Champion Show. Thousands of Paint horses from all over the country compete in over 100 events, including western riding classes, hunter classes, barrel racing, and roping.